WORDS
KAREN KILPATRICK

PICTURES
GERMÁN BLANCO

P.I. BUTTERFLY

GONE GUPPY

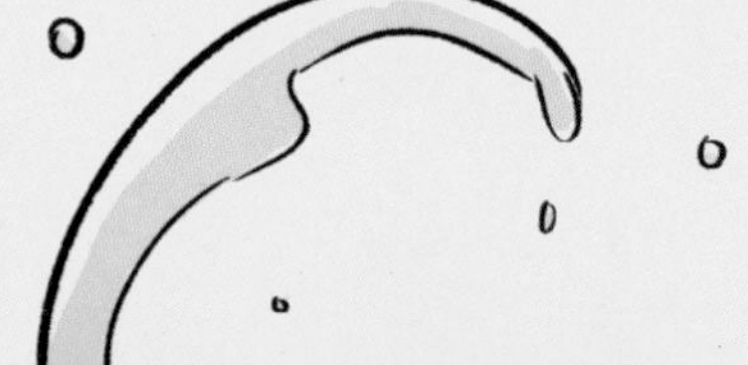

FOR SAGE, MY INSPIRATION FOR P.I.B.
-KK

TO YOUNGER ME, FOR STICKING WITH IT.
-GB

Genius Cat Books

Genius Cat Books

www.geniuscatbooks.com

Parkland, FL

ABOUT THIS BOOK
The art for this book was created with photoshop and illustrator, using a Wacom Cintiq. Text was set in CCMeanwhile, CCBiffBamBoom, BadDog, and American Typewriter. It was designed by Germán Blanco.

Library of Congress Control Number: 2022935089

ISBN: 978-1-938447-46-4

First edition, 2022

Our books may be purchased in bulk for promotional, educational, or business use. For more information, or to schedule an event, please visit geniuscatbooks.com.

Printed and bound in China.

PICTURES
GERMÁN BLANCO
P.I. BUTTERFLY
GONE GUPPY

table of Contents

Good Luck!

CHAPTER 1

THE DISAPPEARANCE

GOOD MORNING, WORLD!

IT'S TIME TO EMERGE FROM MY CHRYSALIS AND FLY INTO THE DAY!
Chrysalis: \chrys·a·lis\ Butterfly version of a cocoon.
IT'S SATURDAY, THE BEST DAY OF THE WEEK.
NO SCHOOL, NO HOMEWORK, NOTHING BUT TIME TO DO MY FAVORITE THING IN THE WHOLE WORLD...

LEARN ABOUT
BUTTERFLIES!
OUCH!
HEY, DID YOU KNOW THAT BUTTERFLIES DON'T FEEL PAIN?
TOO BAD I'M NOT A BUTTERFLY, I WOULD-

AAAAAAHHHH

A SCREAM!
I RUSH DOWNSTAIRS TO SEE WHAT'S WRONG.
IT'S MY LITTLE SISTER, QUINN!

OH NO!
MILI THE FISH IS MISSING!

I SURVEY THE SCENE AND SUSPECT FOUL PLAY.
A GUPPY CAN'T JUST DISAPPEAR BY ITSELF, CAN IT?

YOU HAVE TO FIND HER!

I RUN TO GET MY SUPPLIES.

IT'S TIME FOR...
P.I. BUTTERFLY!!!

THAT'S ME IN CASE YOU DIDN'T KNOW.

CHAPTER 1.5

INTERLUDE

Interlude (noun):
/in·ter·lude/ a break or a pause

I'M PAUSING THIS STORY TO SHARE SOME IMPORTANT FACTS.

A ***P.I.*** (OR PRIVATE INVESTIGATOR) IS LIKE A DETECTIVE.

Train your Pet
A P.I. IS HIRED TO SOLVE MYSTERIES FOR PEOPLE WHO NEED HELP.

PRIVATE INVESTIGATION

HERE'S HOW IT WORKS!

I ACCEPT ALL FORMS OF PAYMENT FOR MY PRIVATE INVESTIGATION CASES:

CANDY,

BUTTERFLY LARVA,

BUTTERFLY ACCESSORIES,

BUTTERFLY NETS,

BUTTERFLY CLOTHES,
BUTTERFLY WINGS
AND CATERPILLAR STUFF, IF YOU HAVE NOTHING ELSE!

SIMPLE, YOU SEE?
YOU MAY ALSO BE WONDERING HOW I BECAME A P.I. IN THE FIRST PLACE.

5 YEARS AGO
WHEN I WAS JUST A LITTLE GIRL, I WAS PLAYING WITH MY DOLL, DOLLY,
WHEN MY NOSE PICKED UP A DELICIOUS SCENT.
I FOLLOWED THE SMELL INSIDE WHERE I DISCOVERED...
A PLATE OF CHOCOLATE CHIP COOKIES!

I GRABBED SOME COOKIES TO SHARE WITH DOLLY BUT WHEN I GOT BACK OUTSIDE, SHE WAS MISSING!
I SEARCHED EVERYWHERE FOR HER,
BUT DOLLY WAS NOWHERE TO BE FOUND.

I DIDN'T KNOW WHAT TO DO,
BUT THEN I NOTICED A
BEAUTIFUL BUTTERFLY...

THAT WAS OBVIOUSLY TRYING
TO TELL ME SOMETHING.

I FOLLOWED THE BUTTERFLY ACROSS MY BACKYARD
WHERE I SAW MY NEIGHBOR'S DOG GETTING READY TO DROP A MYSTERIOUS OBJECT INTO A HOLE.
I GOT THERE JUST IN THE KNICK OF TIME.

THE BUTTERFLY HAD LED ME STRAIGHT TO DOLLY AND SAVED THE DAY!
THAT WAS WHEN I REALIZED BUTTERFLIES ARE SYMBOLS FOR TRUTH AND JUSTICE.
AND I WANTED TO BE JUST LIKE THEM, HELPING PEOPLE BY SOLVING MYSTERIES.

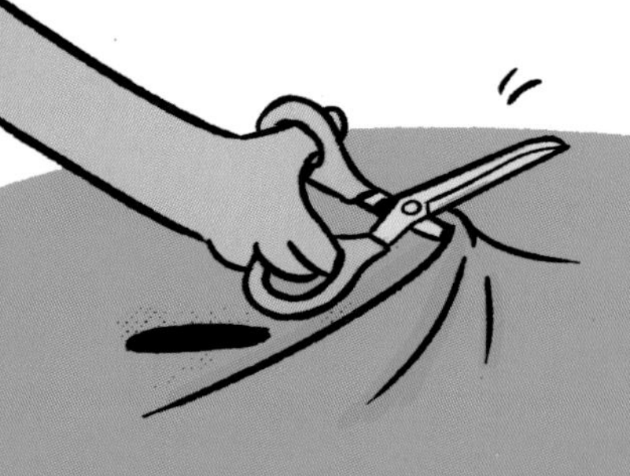
AND SO I BECAME...

P.I. BUTTERFLY

PRESENT DAY
NOW LET'S GET BACK TO THE CASE

SEARCHING FOR CLUES

Perimeter (noun): \pə-ri-mə-tər\ the boundary of an area. In this case, the area around the crime scene!

NEXT, I SEARCH FOR CLUES.

IT'S IMPORTANT TO TAKE MY TIME SO I DON'T MISS SOMETHING IMPORTANT.

HMMMMM, INTERESTING.
2
3
STAY BACK, ALFREDO! DON'T YOU KNOW THAT CHOCOLATE CAN BE DEADLY FOR CATS?
SMACK!
IT CONTAINS A TOXIC AGENT CALLED THEOBROMINE.
Toxic agent = poison!
Theobromine = bad for cats!

FINALLY, I RECORD THE CLUES IN MY BUTTERFLY NOTEBOOK.

CLUES:
1. Chocolate wrapper
2. Spilled fish food
3. Cat hair on the counter and
by the fishbowl

NOW THAT I'VE WRITTEN EVERYTHING DOWN, I'M READY TO INTERVIEW THE SUSPECTS!

CHAPTER 3

THE SUSPECTS

Suspect One:
Mom
Alias: Momma
Age: 100
Address: Home

Appearance: Medium height, medium length hair, medium build.

Opportunity: She's up early every morning to cook breakfast.

Top Secret
Mom
Finger Prints

SHE WAS TIRED OF CLEANING THE BOWL, SO SHE GOT RID OF THE FISH WITHOUT TELLING A SOUL.

WHEN DID YOU LAST SEE MILI?
BUT YOU'RE *ALWAYS* THE FIRST ONE DOWNSTAIRS TO MAKE BREAKFAST. DIDN'T YOU SEE HER THEN?
LAST NIGHT BEFORE BED, I THINK. WHY? AND WHAT'S THIS MESS?!
2
3
Fish n' Chimps
EARLIER THAT MORNING
"WELL, I WENT TO THE PET SUPPLY STORE RIGHT AFTER I WOKE UP THIS MORNING, BUT I GOT TIED UP. SO I HAVEN'T BEEN IN THE KITCHEN YET."

SPEAKING OF BREAKFAST...

I'LL WHIP SOMETHING RIGHT UP, BUT THEN YOU HAVE TO HELP ME CLEAN UP THIS MESS. EGGS OR PANCAKES?

Fish n' Chimps

PANCAKES, PLEASE!
BUTTERFLAP!
I. MUST. STAY. FOCUSED.
ISN'T IT TRUE THAT YOU'RE TIRED OF CLEANING MILI'S BOWL?
YES, IT'S TRUE. YOU KIDS PROMISED TO TAKE CARE OF THE FISH THEN LEFT IT ALL TO ME!
THAT'S WHY I JUST BOUGHT THIS SELF-CLEANING AQUARIUM, SEE?
HISS
Fish n' Chimps

I END THE INTERVIEW EARLY SINCE SHE CLEARLY HAS A VERY IMPORTANT JOB TO DO.
The best for your Fish
AQUA LIFE
LED INCLUDED
2
3

THAT'S WHEN I NOTICE SOMETHING I HADN'T SEEN BEFORE...
2
3
LED

ANOTHER CLUE! I GRAB THE TEA CUP TO ADD TO THE EVIDENCE BEFORE TRACKING DOWN MY NEXT SUSPECT.
2
3

Detention Slip
Tobias
First Name
Room: 201
Made Robot sounds
saying he had no batteries
This must be presented
Miss Philippin
Instructor Signature
TOKEN
NO CASH VALUE

Suspect Two: Tobias
Alias: Toby
Age: Baby
Address: Room 2

Appearance: Messy, dirty.

Opportunity: It was Toby's turn to feed the fish this morning.

MOST WANTED
ONE TICKET
STINKY
Annoyin' Little Brother
finger Prints

MOTIVE:

HE REALLY WANTED A PET GIRAFFE, SO HE GOT RID OF THE FISH WITH A MISCHIEVOUS LAUGH.

LOOKS LIKE YOU MADE A MESS WITH THE FISH FOOD.
WASN'T ME! I WAS IN BED. ASK ANYONE!
ISN'T IT TRUE YOU WANTED MILI GONE SO YOU COULD GET A PET GIRAFFE?
NO! I WANTED TO TRADE ***ALFREDO*** FOR THE GIRAFFE!
UM, JUST KIDDING ALFREDO...

LOOK, A SNAKE!
I TURN AROUND, BUT NOTHING'S THERE.
AND NOW, TOBY HAS DISAPPEARED!

WHAMO!
STOP RIGHT THERE ALFREDO! I HAVE SOME VERY IMPORTANT QUESTIONS FOR YOU!

Suspect Three:
Alfredo
Alias: Furball
Age: ??
Address: The left couch cushion.
Appearance: Orange and fluffy.
Opportunity: Quiet and stealthy, Alfredo could have snuck up on Mili at any time.

Wild Animal
ROAR
FOOD
Homeworks eaten!
Paws

MOTIVE:
ALFREDO LIKES TO EAT FISH, AND MILI WOULD MAKE A WONDERFUL DISH.

WHERE WERE YOU AT THE TIME OF MILI'S DISAPPEARANCE?
MEOW
HEY, WHY IS YOUR FUR WET?
MEOW!
ISN'T FISH YOUR FAVORITE FOOD?
MEOW!
SNATCH!

NOT NOW, ALFREDO, WE CAN PLAY LATER.
IT'S ALMOST LIKE ALFREDO WAS TRYING TO TELL ME SOMETHING...
BUT NOW THAT I HAVE MY MASK BACK, IT'S TIME TO SPREAD MY WINGS AND SOLVE THIS CASE!
MOM
Toby
P.I. Butterfly

CHAPTER 4

THE EVIDENCE

FIRST, I READ OVER MY INTERVIEWS WITH THE SUSPECTS TO SEE IF I CAN POKE HOLES IN ANY OF THE STORIES.

"Poke holes" is a fancy P.I. way to say finding a mistake or a problem.

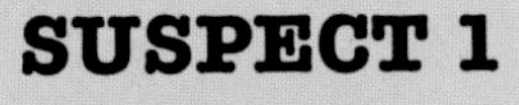

SUSPECT 1

Mama

HER STORY ABOUT THE SNAKES SOUNDED A LITTLE FAKE AND SHE WAS IN A RUSH TO CLEAN UP THE MESS IN THE KITCHEN.

EVIDENCE
FAKE SNAKES
TUFF
WHAT IF SHE WAS TRYING TO DESTROY THE EVIDENCE?!
MOM

SUSPECT 2

Toby

NOBODY ACTUALLY SAW HIM IN BED LIKE HE SAID, WHICH MEANS HE DOESN'T HAVE AN ALIBI. HE ALSO PULLED OFF A SUSPICIOUS ESCAPE FROM THE INTERVIEW.

VERY SUSPICIOUS.
Toby

Alibi (noun): /ˈaləˌbī/ a claim or piece of evidence that one was elsewhere when an act took place.

SUSPECT 3
Alfredo the Furball
A CAT'S BIGGEST WISH IS A FISH DINNER DISH. PLUS ALREDO'S HAIR WAS FOUND ALL OVER THE CRIME SCENE!
Did you know that indoor cats shed all year round?

NEXT, I REVIEW THE PHYSICAL EVIDENCE I COLLECTED FROM THE SCENE.

MY ANTENNA IS PICKING UP SOMETHING IMPORTANT...

THE EVIDENCE SHOWS THAT SOMEONE ISN'T TELLING THE TRUTH!
Toby

TIME TO FLY INTO ACTION AND CONFRONT MY MAIN SUSPECT!

CHAPTER 5

THE TRAIL TO NOWHERE

STOP RIGHT THERE!!!

A CATERPILLAR CAN'T OUTRUN A BUTTERFLY!
TACKLE!!!
THIS SLEEPING BAG WILL HOLD HIM!

THE EVIDENCE PROVES YOU WERE DOWNSTAIRS THIS MORNING AND NOT IN BED LIKE YOU SAID.
Toby
WHAT HAPPENED TO MILI?!

EARLIER THAT MORNING
OK, OK I ADMIT IT! WHEN I WENT DOWNSTAIRS THIS MORNING, THERE WAS NO BREAKFAST. I WAS REALLY HUNGRY, SO I DECIDED TO EAT SOME OF MOM'S CHOCOLATE.
I WAS GOING TO FEED MILI,
BUT HEARD A NOISE AND HAD TO GET AWAY FAST!
CREAK...
HOW'D YOU FIGURE IT OUT?

YOUR MESS LEFT A TRAIL POINTING STRAIGHT TO YOU!
Toby
BUT MILI WAS STILL IN HER BOWL WHEN I LEFT, I SWEAR IT!

HOW DO I KNOW I CAN TRUST YOU?
I'LL PINKY PROMISE I'M TELLING THE TRUTH! NOBODY EVER BREAKS A PINKY PROMISE.

BUT IF TOBY DIDN'T DO IT, WHO DID?

lowfat 2%
MILK
cow milk

CHEERS!
Milk
LOOK, YOU FOUND MY TEACUP!
THANKS!

QUINN WAS THE FIRST TO DISCOVER THE CRIME,
BUT WHAT IF IT WAS HER THE ENTIRE TIME?

CHAPTER 6

A NEW SUSPECT

Suspect Four: Quinn
Alias: Q-tip
Age: Princess Baby

Address: The Unicorn Rainbow room.

Appearance: The girl with 100 hats.

Opportunity: She was found alone with the empty bowl and might have faked her scream to throw me off the trail.

Most Wanted!

lil' princess

finger Prints

SHE NEEDED AN EXTRA GUEST FOR TEA
AND THOUGHT MILI WOULD FIT IN PERFECTLY.

Impede (verb): /im·pede/ to interrupt or slow the progress of something.

QUINN'S ROOM
STEAL
GIVE ME BACK MY HAT!
SORRY, BUT IT'S EVIDENCE NOW.

MOOOOOMMM!!!
UH OH. TIME TO FLUTTER AWAY BEFORE I FLY INTO TROUBLE...!

I HEAD BACK TO MY ROOM TO PLAN MY NEXT STEPS, BUT THERE'S A BIG SURPRISE WAITING FOR ME...

CHAPTER 7

THE CONFESSION

ALFREDO, WHAT DID
YOU DO?!

I THINK ALFREDO WANTS TO CONFESS.

MEOW, MEOW, MEOW...
MEOOOW...

MEOOOW...
MEEEOOOWWW!
OK, OK I GET IT! LET ME RECAP FOR YOU...

EARLIER THAT MORNING
ALFREDO WAS PRACTICING HIS POUNCING SKILLS WITH HIS TOY MOUSE.
MEOW!

HE JUMPED ONTO THE COUNTER, SLIPPING ON THE CHOCOLATE WRAPPER AND KNOCKING OVER THE FISHBOWL!
THWONK!
MILI SPLASHED TO THE GROUND AND....

ALFREDO ATE HER!
MEOW?

NO?
EARLIER THAT MORNING, TAKE TWO.
OK, ALFREDO WAS READY TO POUNCE WHEN...

HE JUMPED ONTO THE COUNTER, SLIPPING ON THE CHOCOLATE WRAPPER AND KNOCKING OVER THE FISHBOWL,

THUNK!

BUT MILI WAS ALREADY MISSING!

CURIOUS, HE FOLLOWED A TRAIL OF WET SPOTS ALL THE WAY TO...
THE UNICORN RAINBOW ROOM,
UNICORN
WHERE HE FOUND MILI AT A TEA PARTY.
AND THEN, WHEN NOBODY WAS LOOKING...

HE ATE HER!
MEOW?

EARLIER THAT MORNING, AFTER THE POUNCING INCIDENT

WHERE HE FOUND MILI, A FISH OUT OF WATER AT THE TEA PARTY!

HE SCOOPED HER UP, AND ...
WAIT FOR ME! I'M COMING ALFREDO!

ALFREDO DROPPED
MILI IN THE TOILET
BOWL!

OH ALFREDO, THAT WAS SOME QUICK THINKING. YOU SAVED MILI!

LOOKS LIKE P.I. BUTTERFLY'S CRACKED ANOTHER CASE!

MEOW...

I'LL BE RIGHT BACK, ALFREDO.
THERE'S ONE MORE THING I HAVE TO DO.

CHAPTER 8

THE TRUTH ALWAYS PREVAILS

Truth is #1!

I HEAD BACK TO QUINN'S ROOM AND KNOCK ON THE DOOR.

QUINN'S ROOM
BUT I ALREADY WENT EARLIER THIS MORNING! AND I FLUSHED, TOO.
COME ON, Q-TIP, THERE'S SOMETHING YOU NEED TO SEE.

IS IT MY HAT?
YOU FOUND MILI!

IS THERE ANYTHING YOU NEED TO TELL ME...?
WELL...

EARLIER THAT MORNING
OK, OK. I INVITED MILI TO MY TEA PARTY AND SHE REALLY WANTED TO COME!

SO I FISHED HER OUT OF THE BOWL AND BROUGHT HER TO THE PARTY.

YOU COULD TELL MILI WAS SUPER EXCITED BECAUSE SHE WOULDN'T STOP MOVING...

BUT THEN SPARKLEFLUFF KNOCKED OVER THE TEA
QUINN'S ROOM
AND I HAD TO GET MORE.
QUINN'S ROOM
WHEN I GOT BACK, MILI WAS GONE!

I RAN DOWNSTAIRS TO SEE IF SHE HAD SWUM BACK TO HER BOWL, BUT IT WAS EMPTY!

AND THAT'S WHEN YOU SHOWED UP...

AFTER YOU LEFT THE ROOM, ALFREDO SAW MILI FLOPPING ON THE FLOOR. SHE MUST HAVE FALLEN OUT OF YOUR TINY TEA CUP! HE SCOOPED HER UP AND BROUGHT HER TO WATER BY DROPPING HER IN THE TOILET BOWL!

GOOD THING HE WAS FAST, BECAUSE GUPPIES CAN ONLY LIVE 3-4 MINUTES OUTSIDE OF WATER.
R.I.P.
MILI
3-4 MINS

I'LL LET YOU OFF THE HOOK THIS TIME, BUT NO MORE TEA PARTIES FOR MILI!
THAT'S OKAY, I FOUND ANOTHER GUEST FOR MY PARTY ANYWAY!

INN'S
OOM
BACK IN QUINN'S ROOM

SMELLS LIKE MOM MADE FOOD FOR MY TEA PARTY!
AND IT LOOKS LIKE IT'S TIME TO COLLECT PAYMENT FOR SOLVING THIS CASE.
GRUMBLE!
COME ON ALFREDO, LET'S GET MILI'S NEW BOWL SO WE CAN GO EAT BREAKFAST!

FLUSH!

DON'T WORRY, MILI, WE'LL SAVE YOU...!

SEWER

THE END

DEAR P.I.-IN-TRAINING:

I WILL CLUE YOU IN ON MY MOST *SECRET* SECRETS OF BEING A GOOD PRIVATE INVESTIGATOR.

ONE

YOU HAVE TO BE CURIOUS. ASK A LOT OF QUESTIONS. A LOT. LIKE **ALL THE TIME.**

two

Be a good listener.

Pay attention to what people are saying to see if there are any holes (something weird, something fishy, something that doesn't make sense) in their stories.

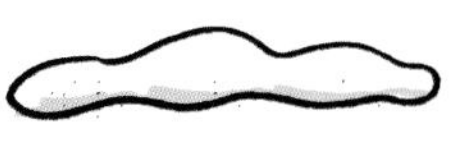

THREE

BE OBSERVANT.

LOOK AT EVERYTHING CLOSELY BECAUSE YOU NEVER KNOW WHAT THE KEY WILL BE TO CRACKING THE CASE!

FOUR
Don't forget to write everything down!
You will need to remember what
everyone said and what you observed in
order to solve the case.
WAIT, WHAT WAS I
TALKING ABOUT?

FIVE
Have patience.
Sometimes it takes a really long time to review the evidence.

You must persevere!

A good private investigator never gives up. Especially when all seems lost.

Persevere (verb): \pər-sə-vir\ continue to do something even when it's really hard.

SEVEN
Don’t forget to focus!
Good private investigators have to be
careful not to get distracted.

EIGHT
AND ABOVE ALL, YOU HAVE TO BE A GOOD PROBLEM SOLVER.
1000
PUZZLE
Solving a mystery requires putting together the clues. Like a puzzle!

P.I. TRAINING

Today we'll work on our OBSERVATION skills.

Throughout the story, how many of these images did you notice?

Poppies
Crocodiles
Snakes
Mice
HOPE TO SEE YOU ON MY NEXT CASE!

Poppies: (6) Crocodiles: (3) Snakes: (5) Mice: (23)

Dear P.I.-in-training,

Hey, it's me, P.I.B.!

I might need your help solving a new case! My best friend (Alexis Leroy) is missing her favorite flower pen. I've already identified and interviewed the suspects, collected the evidence, and taken witness statements.

I have everything you need to crack the case. You would just have to read through the evidence and figure out who took Alexis's pen!

If you're ready to become a junior P.I., just scan this code to learn more!

Scan me!
But my mom says to **always** ask an adult if it's okay, first!

- PIB

P.S. And be on the lookout for my next book, the Birthday Bandit, coming soon!